TUCKET'S GOLD

ALSO BY GARY PAULSEN

TUCKET'S GOLD

◉

Gary Paulsen

A YEARLING BOOK

Published by
Yearling
an imprint of
Random House Children's Books
a division of Random House, Inc.
1540 Broadway
New York, New York 10036

Visit us on the Web! www.randomhouse.com/kids

Educators and librarians, for a variety of teaching tools, visit us at www.randomhouse.com/teachers

---

ISBN: 0-440-41376-1

Reprinted by arrangement with Delacorte Press

Printed in the United States of America

February 2001

10 9 8 7 6 5

OPM

To Maddux,
who lights up lives

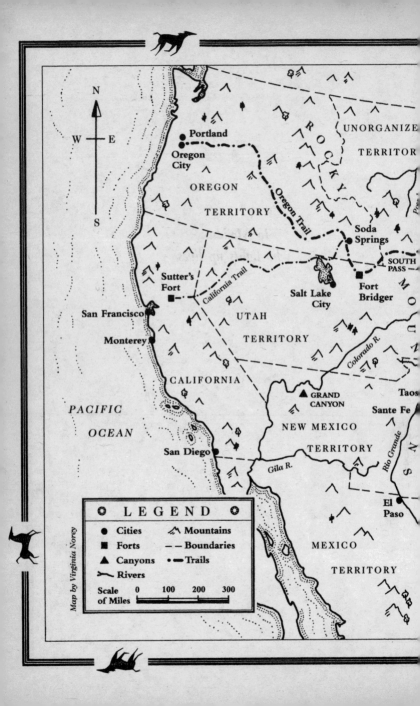

Chapter One

If there was one thing Francis Tucket knew with certainty it was that death, brutal death, was close to taking them.

Dawn was coming and here he was, a fifteen-year-old boy in charge of two children, walking across a sunbeaten, airless plain that seemed to be endless. Francis, Lottie and Billy had no food or water or any immediate hope of getting any, and at any moment a dozen or two of the dirt-meanest men Francis had ever seen in a world *full* of mean men could come riding up on them and . . .

He didn't finish the thought. There was no need. Besides, in surviving Indian fights, blizzards, gun battles and thieves, he had learned the primary rule about danger. It would come if it would come. You could try to be ready for it, you could plan on it, you could even expect it, but it would come when it wanted to come.

Lottie and Billy understood this rule too. He had found them sitting in a wagon on the prairie all alone. Their father had died of cholera and their wagon train had abandoned the family, afraid of disease. Lottie had been nine then, Billy six. Francis hadn't thought he and the children would stay together long—after all, he had to keep searching for his own family. He'd been separated from them over a year before, when Pawnees had kidnapped him from the wagon train on the Oregon Trail. But Francis and Lottie and Billy—well, they were used to each other. They stuck together. Unlike Francis and Jason Grimes, the one-armed mountain man.

Jason Grimes had rescued Francis from the Pawnees and taught him how to survive in the West on his own. Then they'd parted ways.

Until last night. Last night when Grimes had helped them to escape from the Comancheros. The Comancheros were an outlaw band, ruthless, terrifying, inhumanly tough. To escape, Grimes had had to take the packhorses Francis and Lottie and Billy had been riding and lead them off empty, hoping the Comancheros would follow his tracks westward while the three children headed north on foot in the dark of night.

It was a decent plan—it was their *only* plan—and it seemed to be working. As Francis and the two children had moved north in the dark, they had seen the Comancheros ride past them after Mr. Grimes, tracking the horses. The Comancheros had missed the footprints of the children, partly because it was hard to see them and partly because Francis made Lottie and Billy walk in each other's footprints. He came last, brushing out the trail with a piece of mesquite behind him.

But luck was the major factor in the plan. If the Comancheros caught Grimes or even got within sight of him they'd know that Francis and the children weren't with him. They'd turn and come back for the children. Children meant real money because they could be sold or traded into slavery.

Francis knew that brushing out the tracks would only work in the pitch dark of night. In daylight the brush marks themselves would be easy to follow.

"I'm tired." Billy stopped suddenly. "I think we've gone far enough."

Francis frowned. When Francis had first met Billy, the boy wouldn't say a word. And now he'd gone from never talking at all to complaining.

"If they catch us"—Lottie slapped Billy's head so hard Francis thought he heard the boy's brains rattle—"they'll skin you. They'll make a tobacco pouch out of you and let the coyotes have the rest. Now keep walking. If we don't keep moving they'll be on us like dogs, won't they, Francis? On us just like dogs . . ."

Lottie loved to talk, would talk all the time if she had the chance, seemed to have been talking since Francis had found her in that wagon. Lottie would explain every little detail of every little part of every little thing she was talking about so that not a single aspect of it was missed, and she sometimes drove Francis over the edge. Now, as Billy started moving again, Francis picked up the pace, pushed them as hard as they could stand it and then harder, and Lottie didn't have breath left to speak.

Dawn brought the sun and the sun brought heat. Francis and the children were bareheaded and the sun quickly went to work on them. Billy wanted to complain, especially as the morning progressed and there was no water and the sun rose higher and became hotter, but Francis drove them until Billy began to weave. Then Francis handed Lottie his rifle and, pushing her in front of him, he picked Billy up and carried him piggyback, mile after mile, then yard after yard, and finally, step after step.

Lottie saw it first.

"There," she said. "See the spot?"

Francis was near dead with exhaustion. He had hardly slept at all for the two nights before and had been used roughly by the Comancheros in the bargain. He was close to the breaking point as he said, "What spot?"

"There. No, more to the right. On the horizon. It's trees. I'm sure of it. A stand of trees."

They had seen many mirages—images of trees and water that were not there. But Francis looked where she was pointing and saw it instantly. He stopped and set Billy down. The boy was asleep, and he collapsed in a heap, still sleeping. "You're right! Trees. And trees mean water."

5

He turned and studied the horizon. He hadn't been able to look up when carrying Billy and he was shocked now to see a plume of dust off to the west and south. It was at least fifteen miles away, against some hills in the distance. It was so far away that it seemed tiny, but Francis knew it was probably caused by riders, many riders.

Lottie saw him staring.

"Could it be buffalo?" She watched the dust. "A small herd?"

Not here, Francis thought. Not here in this dust and heat with no grass and no water. Buffalo wouldn't be that stupid. "Sure. It's buffalo."

"You're lying." She sighed. "I can tell when you're lying to me, Francis Tucket. It's them, isn't it?"

Francis said nothing but his mind was racing. So the riders were heading back eastward. But why would they be coming back so soon? Had they caught and killed Grimes already? If so they'd be looking for the children. Or had they given up the chase or just seen Grimes and found that he was alone and turned back, still looking for the children? Well, Francis had his rifle. He was ready. He would get two, maybe three of them before they

6

were on him, and maybe that would discourage them. Or they might miss the tracks.

He knew this was a vain hope. There hadn't been a breath of wind to blow the dust over the brush marks he'd left, and undoubtedly they had men who were good trackers, men who were alive because they could track mice over rocks. So the Comancheros would find them and he'd get one or two and then . . . and then . . .

He looked to the trees, which were about two miles away. He could carry Billy there. They could get to the trees in time. Then what? The riders would keep coming back until they came to the place where Francis and the children had turned off, about nine miles back. They would see the marks and turn and start north. Nine miles. The horses would be tired but they would make ten miles an hour. They had to ride maybe twenty miles back to the turn and then nine or ten miles north after the children. He let the figures work through his tired brain. Maybe four hours but more likely three. The riders would be on them in three hours.

Francis and Billy and Lottie would need an hour to make the trees and then . . . and then nothing.

It would all just happen later. He'd get one or two of them and then they'd get him and take the children and nothing would have changed except that a few horses would be very tired and he, Francis, would be dead. If he was lucky. He did not want to think of what they would do with him if they caught him alive.

And as for what would happen to Lottie and Billy—his heart grew cold. But there was something else back there, more than just the plume of dust. There was a cloud. At first it was low on the horizon and showed only as a gray line, so low that Francis almost didn't see it. But it was growing rapidly, the wind bringing it from the west, and as it grew and rose he could see that it was the top edge of a thunderhead.

It didn't *look* like salvation, not at first. He had seen plenty of prairie thunderheads but as he watched it he realized two things.

One, it was growing rapidly, roaring along on the high winds, coming toward them at a much faster rate than the horses of the Comancheros. Two, it would bring rain.

Rain that would ease their thirst and cool their burning bodies and, far more important, rain that

8

might wipe out their tracks, erase everything they had left behind them.

Still, it was a race, and nothing was sure. The clouds had to keep coming to beat the horsemen to where the children's tracks turned north. And it had to rain.

If the clouds turned off or didn't beat the Comancheros or didn't leave rain, then distance was all the children had. They needed to get to the trees and build some kind of defense.

Francis picked up Billy, who was still sound asleep and seemed to weigh a ton. He set off at a shambling walk, abandoning the tedious brushing in their race to get to the trees. Lottie shuffled ahead, carrying the rifle and Francis's possibles bag. She was wearing a ragged shift so dirty it seemed to be made of earth. Her yellow hair was full of dust. Francis wore buckskins, but the children only had what was left of their original clothing and what they'd managed to pick up along the way.

We're a sight, Francis thought. A ragtag mob of a sight.

He looked at the trees and they didn't seem any closer.

He looked at the cloud and it was still building,

though it seemed to be heading off slightly to the south.

He looked at the dust plume and it was still moving on the same line eastward, getting ready to cross their trail.

He looked back to the trees and thought, I would absolutely kill for that old mule we had. But the mule had been taken by the Comancheros.

Chapter Two

They reached the trees just as the edge of the cloud caught up with them.

"Ten more feet and I would have died," Lottie whispered, and sank to the ground.

Francis dropped Billy like a stone—the boy fell without awakening—and studied their location. It was a meandering dry streamed with a row of stunted but leafy cottonwoods along each side. There were also stands of salt cedar, thick and green, and while no water was evident the streambed seemed moist. Francis knew there was water beneath the surface or the trees would have been dead.

"Lottie, scoop a hole there, at the base of that rock."

"You want to start digging, why don't you just go ahead? I have more important things to do than scrape at the old ground."

"Water." Francis was so dry he croaked. "Dig down and let it seep in."

"Oh. Well, why didn't you say so?" Lottie knelt by the rock and started digging in the loose sand with her hands. When she was down two feet, she yelped.

"Here it is! Just like you said, coming in from the sides. Oh, Francis, it's so clear, come see." She scooped some up and drank it. "Sweet as sugar. Come, try it."

Francis knelt and cupped his hand and drank and thought he had never tasted anything so good. But he stopped before he was full.

The wind was picking up now, blowing hard enough to lift dust and even sand, and he could no longer see the dust from the riders. The wind was blowing at the coming thunderheads and he smiled because even if it didn't rain there was a good chance the wind would fill in and destroy their tracks.

By now the thunderhead was over them, dark, so huge it covered the whole sky, and the wind had increased to a scream.

"Over here!" Francis yelled to Lottie. "Beneath this ledge." Incredibly, Billy was still asleep. Francis grabbed the boy and shook him until his eyes opened. "Get over by that rock ledge. Everything is going to break loose—"

A bolt of lightning hit so close Francis felt it ripple his hair, so close the thunder seemed to happen in the same split instant, and with it the sky opened and water fell on them so hard it almost drove Francis to his knees. He had never seen such rain. There seemed to be no space between the drops; it roared down, poured down in sheets, in buckets.

Francis couldn't yell, couldn't think, couldn't breathe. He held Billy by the shirt and dragged him in beneath the ledge that formed the edge of the streambed, away from the trees and out of the wind.

Lottie was there already and they huddled under the overhang just as the clouds cracked again and hail the size of Francis's fist pounded down. One hailstone glanced off the side of his head and nearly knocked him out.

"Move in more," he yelled over the roar of the storm. "Farther back—*move!*"

He pushed against Billy, who slammed into Lottie. They were already up against the clay bank beneath the ledge and could not go farther in. Francis's legs and rear were still out in the hail and took a fearful beating. He doubled his legs up but even so the pain was excruciating and though the large hailstones quickly gave way to smaller ones, his legs were immediately stiff and sore.

The streambed filled in the heavy downpour. Luckily they were near the upstream portion of the storm and so avoided the possibility of a flash flood—which would have gouged them out of the overhang and taken them downstream to drown. As it was, the water came into the pocket beneath them and turned the dirt to mud and soon they were sitting in a waist-deep hole of thick mud and

14

water. And just as soon, in minutes, the rain had stopped, the clouds had scudded away and the sun was out, cooking the mud dry.

Aching, Francis pulled himself into the sun. The children crawled after. Water still ran in the stream but was receding quickly. The hot sun felt good, and Francis wanted to take his buckskin shirt off to hang. But he knew that if he didn't keep wearing it the shirt would dry as stiff as a board.

He straightened slowly, working the pain out of his legs. He looked to the west and smiled.

There would be no tracks after *that*. There might not even be any Comancheros left if the lightning hit their horses, which happened often. Horses seemed to draw lightning. Buffalo too. Francis had seen dead buffalo after a thunderstorm, still smoking from lightning strikes, the meat already cooked and ready to eat. . . . Thinking of roast buffalo made his stomach growl.

"I'm hungry." It was the first thing they'd heard in hours from Billy, finally awake, a standing mudball. "I'm *really* hungry."

"Well, I hope you aren't figuring on meat for a meal," Lottie said, holding up Francis's rifle, "because *this* thing isn't going to shoot."

Francis took the weapon and his possibles bag from her. Both were soaked, so he set to work.

He opened the possibles bag and spread his patch material—mattress ticking—and two cans of a hundred percussion caps each on a rock to dry in the sun. The caps had stayed mostly dry in the tight containers but he knew they fired better when totally dry.

He was surprised to find that the powder was only slightly damp. The powder horn was watertight except for the stopper on the pouring end and it had let in only a drop or two, which had been quickly absorbed by the powder near the spout and hadn't penetrated into the rest of the powder.

He thought of pouring the powder on a rock to dry, just to make certain, but decided against it. It was all the powder he had, maybe enough for eighty or a hundred shots, and one puff of wind would take it all away. The balls themselves were of lead and not damaged. He had about sixty left. The ball mold was of brass and would not rust, though he dried it carefully and set it aside.

He checked his grease pouch and found it still in good shape—the water couldn't do much to grease—and with his gear cleaned and drying he went to work on the rifle. This rifle, a beautiful little Lancaster, had been given to him by his pa on his fourteenth birthday. The same day Francis had been kidnapped.

Francis stared at the rifle. That birthday was so far away—a lifetime ago.

He shook his head and went back to work.

The rush of water had taken the percussion cap off the nipple and he was certain water had worked through the nipple into the powder inside. This meant that the charge would be much reduced in power, if not completely ruined. He put a new cap on the nipple, went to the ledge where they had sheltered from the hail and fired the rifle into the mud. Nothing happened the first time, nor the second. The third time, the caps had burned enough water out so that the remaining powder charge ignited with a dull *phwonk* that drove the ball less than an inch into the mud of the bank.

"I'm getting hungrier," Billy said suddenly.

"Hush now, lizard gut." Lottie cuffed him lightly across the back of the head. "He's working on his tools. Drink water to fill your belly and leave him alone."

17

Francis sat on a rock, which was already dry from the heat of the noonday sun. Using only the small knife from his possibles bag, he took the rifle apart. The patch material was also dry and he ran a slightly dampened patch down the bore of the rifle, then a dry one—using the cleaning rag slot on his ramrod—and when it was completely dried out he set it up so that the sun would shine down the bore as directly as possible.

The walnut stock had been well soaked in oil and bear grease over the years, and the water had not penetrated the wood. But he removed the lock. He wiped it dry and then greased it with a touch of grease from his bag until it cocked and snapped with an almost slick sound.

Finally he used a small nipple wrench from his possibles pouch and removed the nipple, greased the threads and screwed it back in place. Then he smeared a tiny amount of grease on a rag and pushed it through the bore over and over until the rifling was entirely greased and there wasn't a chance of rust.

Finally he put the weapon back together with practiced ease. He measured a charge, poured it down the bore, patched a ball with a greased patch and pushed it down on the powder, pinched a cap so it would wedge tight on the nipple and put the hammer on half cock—the safety notch.

"There." He stood. His shirt was dry and the mud had turned to dust and flaked off the soft leather. His buckskin pants were also dry and still soft and he put the strap of his possibles bag over his shoulder and looked to the sun. "We've got a good five hours of daylight left, maybe six. This streambed moves northwest—which is away from the Comancheros, and it's the way we want to go— so we'll follow it until dark. At least that way we'll have water and—"

"I'm hungry." Billy had locked on the one thought. "And my feet hurt."

"—there's a chance we can run on some meat. All meat needs water and they'll be coming to the streambed to drink. And *all* our feet hurt because we're barefoot." Francis looked down at his feet. The moccasins had long since worn off from walking—they were good for only a few miles in sand and rocks. Yes, his feet hurt too, but they would soon toughen up and get callused.

He started off without speaking and for once Lottie was silent. She followed, dragging Billy by the hand, and the three of them shuffled through the mud and sand and water of the quickly drying stream.

——— Chapter Three ———

They walked along the stream the rest of the day, and though they saw plenty of tracks—deer and rabbit and coyote and some raccoon—they made too much noise for the game to hold position for a shot.

Francis thought of going ahead to hunt, but he hated the idea of leaving the children alone so soon after their brush with the Comancheros. He had despaired of getting any food. But just before dark, when he walked around a curve in the stream, there was a young spike buck standing angled away with its head down, drinking water.

Francis raised and fired without thinking, so fast Lottie yelled and dropped to the ground. She thought somebody was shooting at them.

For a second he thought he'd missed. The deer made an amazing leap to the side, clearing the edge of the streambed and landing above them, a good eight feet up and fifteen over.

But Francis was sure he'd held true and that the ball had gone into the back of the ribs and out the front, through the heart. When he climbed up the side of the stream the buck was lying there on its side, dead.

Francis paused, thanking fate and the spirits and the deer—his stomach growling all the while—and then handed the knife from his possibles kit to Lottie. "Start gutting it and we'll skin it. We'll stay here a day or two and make some moccasins with the green hide. I'm going to look around and make sure we're alone."

At one time Lottie would have objected to getting stuck with the work, but she was too hungry.

Billy looked like he was going to start chewing on one of the deer's feet any second. It was not a time to be squeamish.

Francis reloaded, put a cap on the nipple and studied the surrounding country. He had two worries. One, that somebody might have heard the shot. The Lancaster had a small bore—.40 caliber—and made a fearsomely high, sharp crack when it went off. Still, the sound probably wouldn't carry more than a mile or two—he had fired in the confines of the streambed—but he wanted to make sure that it was a *safe* mile or two.

The second worry was about a fire. They could eat the meat raw—Francis had done so on occasion and he was sure Lottie and Billy would be able to stomach it—but he longed for a full, hot meal. He also needed to melt some grease off the deer to replenish his supply for shooting and cleaning and to work into their feet and moccasin leather. He needed a day down, and the children needed at least a day of rest, maybe more. He had to be able to make a fire and not have it attract any attention.

The country had changed dramatically as they'd moved up the streambed. It had gone from flat desert–prairie to a rolling terrain with outcroppings of rock. Francis climbed one of these outcroppings and sat on the top.

It was about three hours from dark, and the late light cast long shadows from the hills and rocks. He sat quietly and let his mind go blank, let his eyes study. There, a bird wheeling—a hawk—and there, a deer, a mile and more away. To the right, half a mile on, a family grouping of antelope, three of them, and over there, another hawk diving on something, maybe a mouse, and four crows wheeling in a warm draft of air, climbing and tumbling. Two jackrabbits running from one coyote, a half mile to the left. All normal things, all seen and dismissed.

Francis was looking for the other thing, the thing that didn't match the surrounding country. A bit of sharp line, a movement, a curve that didn't follow nature. He swiveled and studied for a full half hour and did not see or hear anything out of place. He gave it another half hour, not moving except to turn carefully, cradling the rifle across his arms. But there was truly nothing out of the ordinary to see or hear or smell or feel.

At last he was satisfied. He stood slowly, his legs

stiff, and moved down the hill and back to where Lottie and Billy were working.

The deer was gutted and the rear partially skinned. It looked like Billy had more blood on him than was in the deer. He looked like a wild animal. Lottie, who had been doing the real work, had only a spot of blood on her cheeks and some on her hands. But she smiled through a cloud of flies—it was hard to believe how many there could be in such a short time in an otherwise empty prairie—and motioned to a stack of wood.

"I had Billy bring in wood. I wasn't sure you'd want a fire but if you did it would be hard to find in the dark and we might fetch a snake were we to grope around without light. I 'collect the time one of my neighbors, I think it was that one named Nancy, she fetched a snake in the woodpile when she was reaching for some firewood in the dark and that was the last time she brought in wood after dark."

Francis waited. Nothing more came. I know I'm going to be sorry for this, he thought, I know I shouldn't do this, I know it's just the worst thing in the whole world to do. "What happened to the snake?"

"She had it by the tail and she took it and whopped it against the side of a chopping block and killed it and then she said, to the snake she said, 'If you want to act like wood you can by jingo *be* wood' and she put it in the stove—it was stiff as a poker because she whopped it kind of hard—and burned it for heat." A deep breath. "Of course that was before she up and took with the ha'nts and could tell about things before they come to be. I remember the time . . . ."

Francis let her go. He was used to the talk; as a matter of fact, he was getting fond of it, and recognized that it was not because she liked to talk so much as because she *saw* things. Saw *everything* there was to see and was very, very smart. She missed nothing. And when there was something to be done—gutting a deer, gathering wood, which he hadn't told her to do but she'd taken care of just on the off chance that he would want a fire—she jumped in and did it.

She finished the story about Nancy while she skinned the deer. Billy helped, and Francis took over when the carcass had to be flopped to get the skin free.

"Get some sharp sticks to cook on," he said. "Green so they won't burn."

When the skin was completely off the carcass he draped it over a bush and cut some meat into strips, meat from the back haunches and the tenderloin down the back. These he laid on top of the ribs to keep them out of the dirt. Then he set about making a fire.

He had no flint or striker, but he did have the rifle and powder. He cut slivers of wood from the dry underside of a wet log and found some dead grass already dry in the hot sun after the rain. He arranged the shredded grass and slivers of wood in a small hollow and sprinkled a bit of powder into a tiny pocket beneath the grass, leaving a thin trail coming back on top of a small flat rock. At the end of the powder trail he put a percussion cap, picked up another stone and struck the cap. It went off with a sharp snapping sound; it lit the powder, whose trail acted as a short fuse that set off the bit beneath the grass. Within three seconds he had a small fire going.

"More wood," he called, and Lottie handed him small pieces until they had a healthy blaze.

"Now the meat . . ." He took a strip of venison, put it on one of the green sticks and held it over the flames, so close that the bottom edge started to burn.

Lottie and Billy did the same and when the meat was hot—well before it was fully cooked—Billy could stand it no longer and ate his piece. He immediately started cooking another, by which time Francis and Lottie had eaten theirs and started on more. They sat that way into the night, eating and cooking, grease in their hair and faces, until a large part of the deer was gone and they were so full they couldn't move.

Francis blinked—a bit of smoke in his eyes—and he was so bone tired that the blink was enough. His belly was full and the fire was warm on his face and his eyes didn't really open after the blink. He rolled onto his side, still facing the fire, saw the children do the same and was instantly, profoundly asleep.

Chapter Four

He slept hard until the sun came creeping into the streambed and warmed his face.

His eyes opened then and he saw the two children lying asleep on the other side of the fire pit. He rose and stood—every muscle in his body seemed to ache—and stretched. Amazing, what a difference a full belly and a drink of water could make.

He picked up his rifle and moved off a bit,

climbed the side of the arroyo and swept the horizon. The sleep had been wrong. In this country, to not keep an open eye but just drop off by the fire was insane, but he had been so tired he couldn't have stayed awake if he'd been lying in broken glass.

Nothing. A clear blue morning sky. Not even a line of clouds. No dust, no horsemen, nothing. It was as if, Francis thought, they were completely alone on the planet.

"We ate most of the deer," Lottie said in back of him, startling him. "Should we get the fire going again and cook the rest?"

"Small," Francis said. "A small dry fire—no smoke. We don't want to attract company. Use dry wood and keep it little. There were some hot coals still there to get it going."

"I know. You don't have to be telling me everything, Francis. I know some things. I know lots of things. There was a man, he came through one time back on the farm and had a list of questions to see could a person know things, and I answered most of them. Although some of the questions were dumb. One was about horses and fish and dogs . . ."

Francis let her ramble and make a fire while he

30

set to work on the hide. Billy was still asleep. They had skinned the deer close so there wasn't any flesh or fat adhering to the hide to scrape off and he stretched the skin to dry in the sun. It would shrink, he knew, but he cut strips from the edge to use for thongs and lacing. He stretched the skin to keep it flat while it dried.

"How long until we can make moccasins?" Lottie asked.

"It should dry enough today if it doesn't cloud up and rain. We can rig something up tomorrow. They'll be made of raw hide but they'll help a bit."

"Good. My poor feet."

Lottie held one off the ground, standing on one foot and tipping the other sole up behind her. Francis could see it was torn and blistered. His were the same and he looked down at Billy, still asleep, and saw that the boy's were the worst of all.

Well, Francis thought, it's a good place to rest. We still have some meat. He marveled that they could have eaten most of the deer, but he'd seen Indians do the same and, after all, they had not eaten properly for days. There's water, he thought, and wood, and we're alone. "We'll stay here two days. Fish me out the deer guts."

"What?" Lottie said.

"The tube guts from the deer. The intestines. Pull them out of the gut pile."

"Is this some kind of joke, Francis? Because if it is . . ."

"Never mind. I'll do it myself." Francis went to the pile of guts where they'd left them. A cloud of flies came up but he took a stick and fished out the intestines. He had seen Indian women clean them out and hang them to dry with a rock for weight so they would become like string for sewing. But they were too far gone and torn apart when he tried to stretch a piece of them. He threw them back. The stomach, lungs, heart and liver were all still there and he knew it was a waste not to eat them. Indians would have eaten them first and saved the meat for later. He'd seen them, and Grimes too, eat buffalo guts and liver raw out of an animal almost before it was dead. But he couldn't bring himself to do it, though it was always wrong to waste part of a kill.

The next day Francis found that making moccasins was more difficult than he'd thought. He had repaired them himself when they had worn out but he'd never made a pair from scratch.

The hide had been stretched and dried for only

one day in the hot afternoon sun. Unfortunately the hair was still on it. Francis used his knife to cut the hair shorter but they didn't have the week it took to throw the hide in a creek to let the hair "slip" out of the skin. For that matter, Francis thought, looking at the streambed, which had further dried up since the rain, we don't have a creek either.

He made the children stand on the hide's skin side and scratched outlines of their feet. He added half an inch around the sides and cut the sole pieces. He did the same for himself, then set all the pieces on the ground, side by side, and looked at them.

"Well," he said. "Well . . ."

"They need walls," Billy said. "They ain't going to work without they have walls."

"You mean sides," Lottie said, "and he *knows* that. Don't you, Francis? You know how to do that, don't you?"

Francis nodded. "Sure."

Of course he didn't, but if he admitted it to Lottie he'd never get another word in. He studied the hide again, wishing he'd spent more time watching the women work and make things when he was a Pawnee captive.

Billy was right. The soles needed walls. Francis cut long strips of hide about two inches wide, cut narrow laces from the remaining hide and, after boring holes with his knife, laced the strips around the soles so they stood upright. Then he cut toe pieces and laced them to the tops of the walls until he had some version of moccasins.

"They look alive," Billy said. "Like they'll eat our feet."

Francis smiled. They did look odd. He hadn't gotten all the hair off, and even the laces were fuzzy. The end result was comical: hair-covered, fluffy, odd ends sticking out all over the place . . .

"They'll break in soon," Francis said. "Let's get walking. I don't like staying here." He couldn't shake the feeling that the Comancheros had ridden past them—well to the south but past them just the same—and would come back for them somehow.

When Francis was finished, they'd been in camp just over two days. In that time the three of them had eaten most of the good meat off the deer, except for some strips they'd dried in the sun. Francis gave the strips to Lottie and Billy to carry, shuffled his feet deep into the green-hide moccasins and set off.

"Which way are we going?" Lottie held back. "Do we have a plan?"

"Northwest. It's the only way to go." In truth they had no choice. Somewhere to the west of them lay a great desert. He had heard people talk of it, and if he took the children there they would certainly die of thirst. East of them lay a whole area ravaged by the war between Mexico and the United States, an area where bandits ruled the land. And south of them . . . well, that was the way to the Comancheros and he had no illusions about their fate if they went that way.

If they went far enough north they would meet up with the Oregon Trail and maybe get on with a wagon train and head west and he could find his family and . . . and . . . and . . .

It was always there, the dream, the hope. But the truth was he could barely remember them. He stopped walking as the thought struck him: he felt close to these two children, felt that Lottie and Billy were more of a family to him than the one he'd lost when he was taken prisoner.

Lottie and Billy had been trudging with their heads down and ran into Francis.

"Why have we stopped?" Lottie pulled at her

moccasins, which were loose and slapped on her feet. "What are you thinking about?"

Francis looked at them and smiled. "Families," he said. "I was thinking about families."

Then he settled his possibles bag, held his loaded rifle loosely and easily in his right hand, the hammer ready on half cock, and started northwest in the easy shuffle he'd learned from the Indians.

It was the only way to go.

Chapter Five

Francis walked well ahead. He did this partly because the other two had shorter legs and were carrying the dried meat and leftover hide, and partly because he could not stop worrying. Some fears were about the Comancheros, but he worried more about water. They were walking up the streambed and had found puddles here and there, but they were drying up fast, and he did not like the prospect of making a dry camp or of going more than one day without water.

Every now and then he would leave the streambed and move up along the higher banks, or go well off to the side and stand on a hill, careful not to kick up dust for anybody to see.

But there was nothing but a wide, half-desert prairie that seemed to stretch endlessly. He would stand, the rifle cradled in his arm, his eyes moving slowly. Waiting, he studied, and he found birds and rabbits and deer. But nothing human.

Toward evening he roamed wide, moving out carefully half a mile on each side of the streambed, looking for tracks or some sign of movement. Nothing.

He came back into the streambed and walked another hundred yards, looking for just the right place, and at length he found a ledge slightly above the bed with an overhang to catch the light and heat from a fire. In front there was a small pool of water, left either by the rain or, more likely, by a seeping spring. He tasted it. Ah! It was sweet.

"Gather wood," he told the children when they came up. "And dry grass for kindling and for beds. I'm going to look for fresh meat."

"Francis," Lottie began, "we know how to make camp. You don't need to tell us." He nodded and moved off.

Francis checked the cap on the nipple of his rifle, pushed it down tightly with his thumb and moved up the bed of the stream. He had seen many tracks of deer and smaller game. It was time to hunt, even though they had enough skimpy meat to keep them going for two more days and Francis could go days more without eating. He also hated to stop this close to where they'd left the Comancheros. But he had to hunt now in case they came into a country with no game. Cover was thinning and he had to think of three mouths and three stomachs instead of just his own. Lottie and Billy couldn't cope with hunger as well as he could.

It would be wrong to say he hunted. He walked up the streambed, passed two does and an older buck, waited until he saw a young buck, aimed and fired. The deer dropped. It was strange, almost like the deer had never been hunted with a gun. They moved off, away from him, but slowly and only for a few yards, and then they stood and looked at him.

He dragged the deer back to where the children

had gathered wood and grass. It was nearly dark and Billy was chewing on a piece of half-dried venison.

"Here," Francis said, "start gutting and skinning and I'll get a fire going."

"Do we need more meat?" Lottie took the knife he handed her and stood looking at the dead deer with distaste. "It seems as if we have enough meat for a couple of days, and we—"

"We are on foot," Francis cut in. "With bad shoes and two people with short legs. If we had horses or even that mule it would be different. We could pack food or take turns riding and cover some ground. On foot we're going to be lucky to make seven or eight miles a day. I stood on a hill and could see close on to twenty miles and believe me, there is nothing out there where we're heading. So unless we come across some horses we need plenty of food and water now. Start cutting while I get a fire going. Billy, you make us some grass beds up on that ledge. It isn't going to rain tonight so we don't have to worry about flooding. Dig back in a bit and watch for snakes."

Francis shredded dry grass, took a double pinch of powder and put it on a flat stone next to the grass, placed a percussion cap next to it and struck the cap with a rock. It snapped and set the powder off; the powder flashed and the grass caught.

He put more grass on it, then small twigs, and soon the ledge and riverbank were lit with a cheery yellow glow. Francis climbed out of the streambed and was pleased to see that neither the flames nor a glow from them showed above the cut bank more than thirty yards away.

He had taken two steps back toward the riverbed when he heard Billy scream.

"Yaaaaaeeeeeee!"

Snake. It was all Francis could think of. Rattlers hunted at night and they denned up during the day. Billy must have dug into a den just when one was getting ready to come out.

Francis ran back to the edge of the bank and jumped into the streambed.

"Ha'nts!" Billy yelled. "There's ha'nts back in there. I hit a cave of ha'nts!"

"What?" Francis stopped next to the ledge. He couldn't see anything. Lottie was there, covered with deer blood, holding the knife.

"There be ha'nts!"

"What is a ha'nt?"

"Ghost," Lottie said. "He saw a ghost. That's what they call ghosts back home."

Francis peered under the ledge. "In there? In the dirt?"

"Look for yourself," Billy said. "*I* ain't going back in there."

Francis peered back beneath the ledge at a slab of limestone. Over countless years the water had cut back beneath it, making a small roofed area perhaps three feet deep. It could not, by any stretch of the imagination, be called a cave. Not even a hole. But just above the recess the recent rain and flooding had cut the earth away, and when Billy had started to work back in to make a bed the loosened earth above the ledge had given way and a clump had fallen out. There, in that clump of earth, shining in the firelight as if suddenly come to life, was a complete human skull.

Francis jerked back. Then his common sense took over. "It's nothing," he said. "Just a skull. Probably some old grave."

"It's a ha'nt!" Billy stared wide-eyed at the skull. "It's full of evil luck."

"Only for the man who was the skull," Francis

42

said. "It looks like his luck ran out. You can see the hole in his head." He turned the skull slightly with a finger and pointed to a small triangular hole in the forehead. "It looks like a lance hit him, or some kind of sharp club or hammer."

"What's that?" Lottie had come closer and pointed.

"What?"

"Up there, in the dirt. It looks like a piece of steel or something."

Francis put more wood on the fire and in the brighter light he poked back carefully into the dirt the skull had fallen from. He found a metal edge and pulled at it. At first it wouldn't move and then suddenly it came, pulling dirt and what seemed to be the rest of the skeleton along with it. Francis found himself holding—he blinked—a steel helmet. It was rusted and tarnished and somehow looked familiar, though at first he could not tell why. It was round, with a steel brim that came to a point in the front and back, and had a steel edge down the middle of the top.

"It's Spanish," Lottie said. "I remember Pa talked about how the Spanish came to this country before the settlers landed back east, and the Spanish had cities and everything out here. He had a book with pictures and I remember a picture of some men wearing hats like this. He was smart, Pa was." Her voice became sad. "I miss him something fierce sometimes."

Francis nodded and they were silent a moment. He looked down at the helmet. "I remember too. My parents had a book in the wagon, and the pictures showed the Spanish had swords and battle-axes. But no guns." He shuddered. "I wouldn't want to be alone in this country without a gun."

"There's more." Billy had gotten over his fear and pointed back into the cavity left by the falling skeleton. "More metal. See it shine?"

This time he was wrong. Francis reached once more into the hole and tugged at a corner of metal. He pulled out a bar that he took to be lead. Then he dug his fingernail into it, or tried to, and knew. Oh no, this wasn't lead. He took the knife from Lottie, for once speechless, and he scraped a corner with the blade. The metal shone brightly in the firelight.

"It's silver," he said softly. "A whole bar of silver."

"There's more," Billy said, reaching back into

the hole. "A whole lot more." He pulled at a metal band and a rotten wooden container fell onto the ground, bars scattering around Francis's feet. Not all of them were silver. He caught the sheen of yellow through the dirt and picked one up.

"Gold?" He almost whispered it.

Chapter Six

"We're rich." Lottie tried to say it aloud but it came out a whisper. "*Look* at it all."

For a moment Francis couldn't move, couldn't think. It had been so long since he'd really considered money. His life had been all powder and lead and hunting and shelter. Money didn't enter into it. He had never had a dream of wealth. All he thought of was getting through the day—sometimes just getting through the next hour—and the constant thought of somehow, someday, some way getting back to his family.

Now this, he thought. It was almost an irritation. Now this . . . as he looked at the bars scattered around his feet. There were four silver bars and five yellowish bars. All crudely cast but in rough rectangular forms. Not big, but big enough. He used the knife again and knelt down and scraped one of the yellow bars and found it softer than the brass of his ball mold. The scraped area emerged a wonderful glistening yellow-gold color.

Yes, he thought. It's gold.

Yes, he thought again. We're rich. And then a third thought came, the first realistic one: the gold and silver didn't mean a thing out here and it was a long way, an incredibly long, dangerous and hard way on foot to anywhere that gold and silver had any true worth.

"I wonder how it came to be here?" Lottie said. "All just in a pile like this."

"Indians," Billy said. "They must have killed him."

"And then buried him?" Lottie snorted. "I don't *think* so."

"There was somebody with him," Francis said.

47

"They had a fight but fought them off, whoever they were. Then they buried this man and—"

"Buried the gold with him?" Lottie shook her head. "Why would they do that?"

"—and buried the gold for the same reason we have to rebury it. It's too heavy to carry. Go ahead, pick one of them up."

Lottie hefted one of the bars. "It must weigh close to fifteen pounds."

"And the silver weighs almost as much. Nine bars times fifteen pounds—that's going on a hundred and thirty-five pounds. Even breaking the nine bars between us we can't carry it far."

"I could try," Billy cut in, his eyes shining as he stared at the bars. "We ought to give it a really *good* try."

"No." Francis shook his head. "We wouldn't make five miles and believe me, we have a lot more than five miles to go before we're out of this godforsaken flatland."

"So what do we do?" Lottie asked.

"We take some of it. Two bars of gold. Then we bury the rest in a different place and we mark it well so we can find it again. We head north until we can buy some horses and we come back for the gold."

Chapter Seven

w many are there?" Lottie stared down at

cks.

re than five," Francis said. "The tracks run

. And they're fresh, since the rain three days

be only a day old." Lottie looked hard at

had walked less than four miles before

cross the tracks. It had been a soft morn-

"We share it?" Billy looked up.

Francis nodded. "Share and share alike. A third each."

Billy smiled. "How much rock candy can I buy with my share?"

Lottie shook her head. "We'll talk about how you're going to spend it later. Help me with the deer. We have to clean it and strip it and hang the meat to dry. And we have to bury this poor man again."

"Bury him?" Billy looked down. "He's nothing but a few bones and some hair."

"He was a real person and he should get a real burial, same as anybody, isn't that right, Francis?"

Francis nodded. "We have to hide all this again so we can find it when we come back, and that includes burying the man. But not here, not here . . ." He clambered up the edge of the streambed and studied the surrounding terrain for a moment in the darkness.

There was a small depression near three large boulders, the depression in the center of imaginary lines drawn from all three stones. X, Francis thought, marks the spot—or a three-legged X.

"We'll bury him in here." He moved to the depression. "The ground is soft and we can find it again."

"We can dig with these." Billy came up holding a sword in one hand and the old helmet in another. They were rusty—the helmet had a couple of small holes where the rust had eaten through—but the sword was in surprisingly good shape. The blade was short, perhaps two and a half feet, and wider than Francis would have thought. The sword he had seen in the book had a long thin blade, very sharp, with a basket handle. This one had merely a crosstree to protect the hand, and the blade was more like a long sticking knife.

But Billy was right. It would make a good digging tool.

"Start digging," Francis said. "Lottie and I will work on the deer meat."

They had a small fire and Francis hung strips of meat on green sticks over the fire to cook. When they were done and still hot he took some up to Billy, who was digging away, loosening the dirt with the sword and scooping it with the helmet.

It was hard dark now, but a full moon had risen and it threw so much light that it was easy to see where to dig.

"That's close to enough," Francis s
was waist-deep on Billy and about thr
"It can't wash out here and the wind
dirt away down low like this."

Billy put the sword and helmet as
the edge of the hole, chewing the
handed him. "Ain't it strange?"

"What?"

"He was rich, that man. He came
he was rich and somehow died so
spend it. Then we come along an
and now we're rich."

Somewhere off in the distance a
short yips followed by a long hig
answered, mimicking the tone
around the prairie in the moon
but did not say what he knew v
were a long way from being
money. There were many thing
to make them wind up like th
in a hole in the ground.

He shook the feeling off.
Lottie and bury him and hid
lot of work to do."

"H
the tra
"M
togethe
ago."
"May
Francis.
They
coming

ing. The weather had remained clear but somewhat cooler—perfect for walking—and the moccasins were proving to be better than they looked. They had used part of the hide from the second deer to make a crude backpack for the two bars of gold. Billy had cut a strip to hold the sword at his side, though he was so short that if he didn't watch it, the tip dragged in the dirt.

Francis had moved out beside the streambed a few hundred yards, so Lottie, who was in the lead, had come upon the tracks and called for him.

"Horses?" she had said, and pointed. Billy had crouched down to look.

Francis nodded.

"With riders?"

"It's hard to tell."

"I thought you could track."

"I can."

"They don't have shoes," Lottie said now.

"Maybe they're wild horses and we could catch one or two or even three."

Francis had been thinking along the same lines, only a bit more realistically. Unshod horses were not necessarily wild. Indians did not shoe horses, nor were most of the Comancheros' horses shod, except for those they had stolen with shoes on. And catching wild horses wasn't that easy either. There was a reason they were called wild.

But Francis had learned from Mr. Grimes, the mountain man, who in turn had learned by studying wolves and coyotes, that you always watched everything; and when something came along that was different, you investigated it.

Francis had no intention of running into Indians or Comancheros and didn't have a clue about how to catch wild horses. But it was still very interesting that suddenly, in the midst of this flat, grassless plain, the tracks of five or ten horses came in from the side and moved up the streambed ahead of them.

Francis knelt to examine the tracks more closely and found one, with a slight crack in the forward rim of the hoof, that he could identify and study without confusing it with the others.

They were not moving fast, not even trotting. More strangely still they seemed to be moving in a tight group. There was very little space between the tracks and now and then they stopped or moved off to the side a bit and he could see where they had been chewing at small clumps of bunchgrass.

That was a good sign. Ridden horses were not allowed to stop at every little bit of grass. Maybe they were wild . . . but that didn't explain why they stayed in such a tight group. A single horse never went off to the side to nibble—it was always the whole group.

"We'll follow them," he said after a few moments. "They're going our direction anyway. But keep it quiet in case we come up on them."

And so they walked most of the day, moving quietly, taking turns carrying the pack with the gold. The thirty pounds felt heavier and heavier as the day progressed. They peered around each curve in the streambed as they came to it, and it was nearly evening when Francis, who was walking in the lead, froze and held up his hand to stop Billy and Lottie. He'd seen something, a slight movement. He motioned them to move off to the sides of the streambed and wait for him and he made his way around one bend, then another, and when he came to the third curve, a sharp angle to the left, he saw them.

There were six of them. All small Indian ponies, tied together. Or they'd once been tied. Now they were more or less tangled together in a clump.

Francis stopped and studied them, trying to see how it could have happened. They looked rough, muddy, their hair matted and tangled, and some were bleeding from small wounds. But none seemed to have any broken bones; none was dragging a leg.

But where had they come from, and how could they have managed to get this far (however far it was) without killing each other?

They saw him almost at the same moment he saw them and another strange thing happened. Two of them seemed startled and shied slightly, started to run away, but they were all held by leather-rope halters and some kind of picket line that had become so wrapped and crossed that, though the two wanted to run, they were held back by the other four, which were trying to get a drink from a nearly dried-up pool. One of those ponies actually seemed to want to come toward Francis.

He approached them, walking slowly, keeping his arms still and the rifle down at his side so it wouldn't appear to be a stick or club. They all watched him now, but even the shy ones didn't move away. Wherever they had come from, they certainly weren't wild. Their ears were up—filled

"We share it?" Billy looked up.

Francis nodded. "Share and share alike. A third each."

Billy smiled. "How much rock candy can I buy with my share?"

Lottie shook her head. "We'll talk about how you're going to spend it later. Help me with the deer. We have to clean it and strip it and hang the meat to dry. And we have to bury this poor man again."

"Bury him?" Billy looked down. "He's nothing but a few bones and some hair."

"He was a real person and he should get a real burial, same as anybody, isn't that right, Francis?"

Francis nodded. "We have to hide all this again so we can find it when we come back, and that includes burying the man. But not here, not here . . ." He clambered up the edge of the streambed and studied the surrounding terrain for a moment in the darkness.

There was a small depression near three large boulders, the depression in the center of imaginary lines drawn from all three stones. X, Francis thought, marks the spot—or a three-legged X.

"We'll bury him in here." He moved to the depression. "The ground is soft and we can find it again."

"We can dig with these." Billy came up holding a sword in one hand and the old helmet in another. They were rusty—the helmet had a couple of small holes where the rust had eaten through—but the sword was in surprisingly good shape. The blade was short, perhaps two and a half feet, and wider than Francis would have thought. The sword he had seen in the book had a long thin blade, very sharp, with a basket handle. This one had merely a crosstree to protect the hand, and the blade was more like a long sticking knife.

But Billy was right. It would make a good digging tool.

"Start digging," Francis said. "Lottie and I will work on the deer meat."

They had a small fire and Francis hung strips of meat on green sticks over the fire to cook. When they were done and still hot he took some up to Billy, who was digging away, loosening the dirt with the sword and scooping it with the helmet.

It was hard dark now, but a full moon had risen and it threw so much light that it was easy to see where to dig.

"That's close to enough," Francis said. The hole was waist-deep on Billy and about three feet across. "It can't wash out here and the wind can't blow the dirt away down low like this."

Billy put the sword and helmet aside and sat on the edge of the hole, chewing the meat Francis handed him. "Ain't it strange?"

"What?"

"He was rich, that man. He came along here and he was rich and somehow died so he never got to spend it. Then we come along and find his body and now we're rich."

Somewhere off in the distance a coyote wailed—short yips followed by a long high note. Another answered, mimicking the tone. Francis looked around the prairie in the moonlight and thought but did not say what he knew was the truth. They were a long way from being able to spend the money. There were many things that could happen to make them wind up like the Spaniard, wind up in a hole in the ground.

He shook the feeling off. "Come on, let's get Lottie and bury him and hide the gold. We have a lot of work to do."

51

Chapter Seven

"How many are there?" Lottie stared down at the tracks.

"More than five," Francis said. "The tracks run together. And they're fresh, since the rain three days ago."

"Maybe only a day old." Lottie looked hard at Francis.

They had walked less than four miles before coming across the tracks. It had been a soft morning. The weather had remained clear but somewhat cooler—perfect for walking—and the moccasins were proving to be better than they looked. They had used part of the hide from the second deer to make a crude backpack for the two bars of gold. Billy had cut a strip to hold the sword at his side, though he was so short that if he didn't watch it, the tip dragged in the dirt.

Francis had moved out beside the streambed a few hundred yards, so Lottie, who was in the lead, had come upon the tracks and called for him.

"Horses?" she had said, and pointed. Billy had crouched down to look.

Francis nodded.

"With riders?"

"It's hard to tell."

"I thought you could track."

"I can."

"They don't have shoes," Lottie said now.

"Maybe they're wild horses and we could catch one or two or even three."

Francis had been thinking along the same lines, only a bit more realistically. Unshod horses were not necessarily wild. Indians did not shoe horses, nor were most of the Comancheros' horses shod, except for those they had stolen with shoes on. And catching wild horses wasn't that easy either. There was a reason they were called wild.

But Francis had learned from Mr. Grimes, the mountain man, who in turn had learned by studying wolves and coyotes, that you always watched everything; and when something came along that was different, you investigated it.

Francis had no intention of running into Indians or Comancheros and didn't have a clue about how to catch wild horses. But it was still very interesting that suddenly, in the midst of this flat, grassless plain, the tracks of five or ten horses came in from the side and moved up the streambed ahead of them.

Francis knelt to examine the tracks more closely and found one, with a slight crack in the forward rim of the hoof, that he could identify and study without confusing it with the others.

They were not moving fast, not even trotting. More strangely still they seemed to be moving in a tight group. There was very little space between the tracks and now and then they stopped or moved off to the side a bit and he could see where they had been chewing at small clumps of bunchgrass.

That was a good sign. Ridden horses were not allowed to stop at every little bit of grass. Maybe they were wild . . . but that didn't explain why they stayed in such a tight group. A single horse never went off to the side to nibble—it was always the whole group.

"We'll follow them," he said after a few moments. "They're going our direction anyway. But keep it quiet in case we come up on them."

And so they walked most of the day, moving quietly, taking turns carrying the pack with the gold. The thirty pounds felt heavier and heavier as the day progressed. They peered around each curve in the streambed as they came to it, and it was nearly evening when Francis, who was walking in the lead, froze and held up his hand to stop Billy and Lottie. He'd seen something, a slight movement. He motioned them to move off to the sides of the streambed and wait for him and he made his way around one bend, then another, and when he came to the third curve, a sharp angle to the left, he saw them.

There were six of them. All small Indian ponies, tied together. Or they'd once been tied. Now they were more or less tangled together in a clump.

Francis stopped and studied them, trying to see how it could have happened. They looked rough, muddy, their hair matted and tangled, and some were bleeding from small wounds. But none seemed to have any broken bones; none was dragging a leg.

But where had they come from, and how could they have managed to get this far (however far it was) without killing each other?

They saw him almost at the same moment he saw them and another strange thing happened. Two of them seemed startled and shied slightly, started to run away, but they were all held by leather-rope halters and some kind of picket line that had become so wrapped and crossed that, though the two wanted to run, they were held back by the other four, which were trying to get a drink from a nearly dried-up pool. One of those ponies actually seemed to want to come toward Francis.

He approached them, walking slowly, keeping his arms still and the rifle down at his side so it wouldn't appear to be a stick or club. They all watched him now, but even the shy ones didn't move away. Wherever they had come from, they certainly weren't wild. Their ears were up—filled with burrs and mud, but up—and they studied him with interest as he moved toward them.

Twenty feet away he stopped again.

"Easy." He spoke low, almost whispered, but did not hiss. "Easy, easy, ea . . . sy . . ."

They held their position. In the end he walked right up to them, held out his hand, took the chin cord on the halter of a compact pinto. Francis grinned when the pinto nuzzled his shoulder.

"You're all sick of this, aren't you?"

Clearly they were trained and just as clearly they were monumentally tired of being tangled in a six-horse knot. They stood gently while he leaned his rifle against a small tree and untangled them, one by one, tying each horse to the tree when he got it loose.

"Oh my, Francis, look what you've found."

Lottie and Billy came up and even that didn't bother the ponies. "Where did they come from?" Lottie moved to the pinto and began untangling its mane and forelock, taking the burrs out of its ears.

"I'd say Indians," Francis offered. "Except that I don't know if there are any around here. They might be from the Comancheros but it's a long way to their camp—unless they broke away from a moving band. Either way I figure they were picketed and pulled loose in that storm, still all tied to the picket line. They must have panicked and run a distance—probably still driven by the storm—and then kept moving in a clump."

"Comancheros." Billy looked over his shoulder. "They could be tracking the horses."

"Could be." Francis nodded. "But that was a powerful rain. Any tracks were wiped out, and even a Comanchero couldn't track in pure mud. Besides, if they were being followed it stands to reason they would have been caught by now, moving as slow as they were."

"So they're our horses." Lottie smiled.

Francis nodded. "We ride, at least for now." He smiled back at her. "Which one do you want?"

Chapter Eight

They spent that night and the next full day working on the horses. It was one thing for Francis to say they'd ride, another to make certain they could.

The ponies were in a slightly weakened condition at first, and perhaps that was for the best. The pinto still managed to throw Francis twice. Lottie took a small white mare with a circle around one eye, and Billy took a muddy gray pony because he said it reminded him of the mule and he missed the mule.

"Where'd you get that old mule anyway?" Lottie asked. "You never told us."

"Two men named Courtweiler and Dubs came on me and stole everything I had and left me the mule."

"Well." Lottie turned to look at Francis. "I'll bet you fixed those crooks!"

"The mule helped," Francis said. "But that's another story."

Luckily only the pinto bucked. The rest needed care. Francis used some of his deer grease to treat the cleaned cuts and bruises so the flies wouldn't get into the wounds, and spent the rest of the day making usable jaw bridles and reins out of the braided picket lines and halters.

They picked one other horse, a reddish mare, for a packhorse, though they had no true pack to put on her back. They tied the horses to the tree for the two nights they were camped and Francis slept at the base of the tree to be ready in case something frightened them.

At dawn the next morning Francis shook the other two awake. "We're leaving. Come on." They ate cold cooked meat and before true light they headed out, back in the direction from which they'd come, for the rest of the gold.

Francis led at first, riding the pinto and pulling the pack mare with an eight-foot piece of picket line. They climbed out of the streambed and onto the flat of the prairie. He and the pinto had worked out their differences and he found the small horse quick and responsive, answering to knee pressure, so he could steer with his legs and keep his hands free.

"What about the two extra horses?" Lottie followed Francis, and Billy brought up the rear on his gray.

"Enough is a feast," Francis said. "We can't lead them all the time so they're on their own. But I think they'll follow."

And he was right. They fell in behind Billy and walked along as if led.

Francis and the children found that the Spaniard's new burial site had not been bothered. They used Billy's sword—he would not let anybody else carry it—to dig up the gold and silver.

They put it on the pack mare, balancing it on either side in deerskin pouches. There was no cinch and at first the packs would not stay on. Lottie figured out a way to tie it into the mare's mane to keep it centered. Francis took some of another piece of the braided rope that had held the ponies and looped it beneath the mare's belly to keep the packs tied down. It was not truly a cinch but it kept the packs from flopping or coming loose.

They started north again late in the afternoon and by dark they were passing their camp of the previous night.

As before, they began with Francis in the lead. But in time he handed the pack mare over to Lottie and began to range, moving left and right of the centerline of their march.

It felt wonderful to be riding again. The pinto was a good horse and with a little grass and rest and water would be a great one. They had meat left from the last kill, enough for two more days, and now they could cover thirty miles and more a day.

At dark Francis came back to the creek bed where some small cottonwoods stood. They tied the horses to trees, each separately, and gathered wood and cooked meat and ate until they were full. They had to dig a seep pool for water—the stream was dried up—but the water was sweet and there was plenty for all three of them and the horses.

Francis then made a circuit on foot with his rifle, moving out half a mile in the dark, and could not see any sign of light on the horizon or from their own fire.

He had put on a good face for Lottie and Billy, but he was worried. If the ponies had come from the Comancheros, they would be tracking them. But there was no indication that anybody was coming and so he went back to the fire just in time to hear Lottie finish what had apparently been a long story about horses she had known back home.

Billy was sound asleep, and Francis curled up near the tree by his pinto, his rifle in his arms. Soon all three were asleep and there was no sign, not a single indication, that on the following morning Lottie would find the castle in the clouds.

——— Chapter Nine ———

It was strange that Lottie was the one to see it first. She had just been telling about a book she'd read, or somebody had read, that had men fighting with swords, huge swords as tall as the men, and the men lived in castles . . . when she looked up and said, "Like that one up there."

And sure enough there was a castle, or something that looked so much like a castle it didn't matter. It was far off on the horizon, or floating above the horizon, with blue daylight showing beneath the castle and beneath the earth it stood on. It appeared to be made of red sandstone, with buildings on top made from reddish earth and a tower at each end.

"Look close," she said. "You can see the people."

They had been riding close together and at first Francis and Billy couldn't see what she meant. But when they moved their heads closer to Lottie's line of sight the castle jumped into focus. And she was right. Francis could see small figures moving, along the roof or the top of a wall, and around the wall at the base and off to the side was a field of what seemed to be corn, dried and golden.

"It's a mirage," Francis said. "We've seen them before."

"Not like this one," Lottie said. "Not a castle. And not this close."

"A mirage doesn't have to be far away. Mr. Grimes told me once he saw a mirage of a sailing ship on an ocean while he was washing his face in a stream."

"But the people." Lottie pointed. "You can see them so clear. . . ."

They rode in silence for a time—a strange state

for Lottie—and Francis had to agree with her. Mirages usually didn't last long, or they wavered in the light, or shimmered and disappeared. This one did none of those things. Instead the light beneath it narrowed and vanished until the structure was clearly connected to the ground and then it started to grow as they rode through the day, higher and higher until even Francis had to acknowledge that it wasn't a mirage at all but a real castle.

Except that as they grew nearer it became clear that it wasn't a castle so much as a small town on top of a butte.

And with that knowledge Francis realized that he was leading two children and a packhorse carrying a fortune in gold toward a strange village on a strange mountain filled with strange people who might not be friendly.

When evening caught them they were still a good ten or twelve miles from the butte and Francis dropped into a small gully filled with brush and salt cedar and tied the horses.

"We'll make a cold camp. No fire. No cooked meat. Dig a seep hole for water. As soon as it's dark I'm going to move a little closer and take a better look at that place."

"It's a castle," Billy said. "Lottie was right."

"No, Billy," she said. "It's a town on a mountain. I just thought it was a castle."

"Still. They'll have food and water and maybe candy we can buy with the gold. I think we ought to get up there and see if they've got a store."

Francis smiled, though it was lost to the others in the gathering dark. They ate some small pieces of cooked, partly dried venison, and then Francis settled them in, and walked off into the dark.

He set a good pace for two hours and covered five or six miles. Then he slowed a bit and walked another four miles in two more hours. He had been moving in a streambed—dozens cut the prairie surface—and so could not see what was in front, but after walking what he thought might be ten miles he pulled himself up to the edge of an arroyo and took a look.

He was surprised to see that he was quite close to the butte. The moon helped him to see the small adobe houses. They had a soft, curved beauty in the moonlight, and here and there he saw the light of a fire coming through an opening between two houses. There were no lanterns, nor did there appear to be light from candles or anything like a window. He didn't see a horse herd. But there were several fields of corn plants, dry and apparently harvested last fall, and his mouth watered at the thought of corn bread and gravy to go with the venison. . . .

A sound stopped his dream. A soft sound, close, something brushing, no, some sound he'd heard before. Something sliding. Really close. Not sliding either, more slithering . . .

The snake hit him just as he realized what it was and saw it in the moonlight. It didn't rattle, though it was a good four feet long and had close to a dozen rattles. Francis's head had been just over the top edge of the arroyo and his upper right arm lay along the dirt as he held himself there, and the snake hit the muscle in his right arm, down from the shoulder about four inches.

He had some good luck to go with the bad. He was wearing his buckskin and so the fangs did not get in as deep as they might have. And the snake could have hit his neck instead of his arm, which would have killed him pretty quick.

But the fangs did get through into his arm and the snake dropped a heavy dose of venom.

"Ahhh . . ."

Francis fell back into the streambed, six feet down, and for a second raw panic took him. Jumbled images and words. Stupid, he thought—Grimes had told him once that Apaches didn't like to move at night because the snakes hunted then. He knew that. Should have been more careful. Stupid way to die. Couldn't cut up on his shoulder, couldn't get at it to suck it anyway; too far back to Lottie and Billy. He'd never make it.

The pain was immediate and intense: his whole shoulder was on fire.

How long?

Minutes. He'd heard somewhere that maybe half an hour was all it took. And the bite was high on his body. The poison would reach his brain soon. Or his heart.

He could lie down and die right here or he could fight to live. To do that he needed help, somebody to cut the wound, bleed it, poultice it or suck it. Soon. He had to get help. The village.

His mind was fuzzing now, everything becoming blurred as the pain drove him into shock and the venom worked into his system.

He had to keep moving. Make it to the town on the butte. Keep his legs moving. Not running, had to keep it even, keep his blood from pumping hard and carrying the poison, but keep moving.

Colors now, in flashes. He stopped for a moment and vomited. He thought how silly it was to waste all the venison he'd just eaten.

His arm and shoulder were on fire and he kept seeing visions. Lottie and Billy in the wagon. Billy riding the mule backward. More colors. Gold. Gold bars and silver bars and then a sun exploding in his brain, then going out and out, and he was falling now, first to his knees and almost down before somebody was there, a strange-looking man in a strange costume. Not a man, a demon, no, a wild beast with a mask with bulging eyes there in front of him making sounds he couldn't understand.

"Help . . ." Francis tried to speak to the monster. "Snakebit. Shoulder. Two children. Help . . ."

But all that came were more words he couldn't understand and then he was sinking to the sandy floor of the arroyo, first to his knees and then over on his face and then there was nothing.

Chapter Ten

He could not say if he was alive or dead. It was a dream that became a nightmare, back to a dream, and then to another nightmare peopled with strange beings and spirits, and in it all, through it all, there was horrible pain and sickness.

Later he couldn't remember much—and for that he was thankful. Snatches of scenes came. Lottie was there in front of him, and Billy, and then somebody was turning him over and then there was horrible pain in his shoulder and then something with two heads and corn leaves for hair was looking down at him and saying something he couldn't begin to understand, and then he was sweating, pouring more sweat than he ever had in his life, and something hot was going down his throat, hot and thick and sweet and then salty and then finally, for what could have been an hour or a day or the rest of his life, he went back into nothingness, which at last turned into sleep.

He did not awaken as much as become reborn. His eyes opened the smallest crack and he saw or thought he could see a blurred fence in front of him and that didn't make any sense at all because at the same moment he knew he was flat on his back on some kind of blanket. Ceiling. It was a ceiling with round timbers covered with a latticework of smaller limbs and willows. He was looking up at a ceiling. But how . . . when?

His eyes swiveled slightly to his left and he saw Lottie's face. She was sitting on the floor with her face lying on the bed and was sleeping fitfully. He could see her eyelids fluttering. There was light coming through a small doorway that dimly lit a small room not over ten feet square. He was on a bed made of willows in one corner of the room away from the door opening and for what seemed a very long time he could not think on where he was or how he came to be there. He decided he wasn't dead—he didn't think Lottie would be there if he was dead—but at first he couldn't understand how he'd come to be in a room. How could a room be in the prairie?

Then he remembered the town on the butte with the small adobe houses and he knew. "How did I get here?" He said it aloud, or tried to. What came out was a cross between a crow's rasping caw and a hissing whisper.

It was enough to awaken Lottie. "Francis? Are you talking? Did you say something? Oh, Francis, was that really you? I've been so worried these past two weeks that you were going to die and I would have to live without you that—"

"Two weeks?" That came out better. Actual words, but still rasping and choked off.

She wiped her eyes and sat up and nodded. "Billy will be so glad. He's out hunting rabbits with Two Toes—"

"Hunting?"

"Don't worry, he didn't take your rifle. Honestly, if you asked for that gun once you asked for it a hundred times. I'd bring you the rifle and you'd hold it in your arms like a baby or something and go back to sleep. If I took it away you would wake up and ask for it and go back to sleep holding it. Billy is hunting with a bow Two Toes showed him how to make. I swear, he's been running with that boy so much I think he's turned Indian. He can hit a running rabbit with that thing. They have contests, all the boys, and the winner gets the other boys' arrows to use. Billy must have had close to a hundred and fifty arrows before they quit shooting with him. Then he started hunting and it was him brought in all the fresh rabbits for you—"

Francis held up his hand. "Too fast. Go back. I guess we're in the village on the butte—an Indian village. But . . . how did I get here?"

"Oh. Well, I don't know it all because I still can't talk to them very well because they haven't got a handle on English and I can't get my tongue around their words. Billy has learned to rattle with them, or at least with Two Toes—that's a boy he's gotten to be friendly with—but all *they* talk about is hunting and girls—"

"Just what you know. Tell me what you know."

74

"Billy and I were waiting with the horses when six men come out of the dark and took hold of us."

"Took hold?"

"Not in that way. Not in a bad way. Although Billy had a pretty good go at them with his sword when they first came out of the dark. But they kind of wrapped him up and then they stopped and made signs that they were peaceful and had smiles and motioned that we should come with them. They let us ride the horses but *they* didn't ride. They trotted along beside us as fast as the horses moved. And they didn't take the pack either, though you could tell they were curious at how heavy it was. When we got here you were already on this bed and there were two old women and a medicine man working on you. I swear, I didn't know *what* to think. It was getting light when we got here and even as dark as it is in here I could see you were in a bad way.

"I didn't know why at first and thought they must have hurt you but then they showed me the marks on your shoulder and I knew you were snakebit. They let me stay with you but they wouldn't let me make none of my spit-and-mud poultice to draw out the poison. It's a shame too;

75

I had Billy drink water and spit in a gourd all day. We must have had close to a quart. But they wouldn't have it—they used some junk they made up with water and leaves—so it all went to waste."

"They saved me?"

"Well, them and me and Billy. Billy hunted rabbits and we've kept a clay pot of rabbit stew to mix with the corn gruel they give you."

"They must have carried me here from where they found me."

Lottie nodded. "And there's been at least one old woman with you all the time. They fed you and cleaned you and all but I think they were really just here to keep me from using my spit-and-mud poultice. I tell you, I saw a man bit by a copperhead back home and he was up in two days, not two weeks. He went to a dance and danced the reel all night not four days after he was bit. Of course he was dead a week later but that was because he tried to steal a team of mules and somebody up and shot him and couldn't rightly be blamed on the poultice not working."

"They stayed with me?"

Another nod. "Until this morning. They turned you over and looked at your shoulder and one of them nodded to the other one and they left. I thought they had given up. Oh, Francis, I was so sure you were going to die. . . ."

"I thought I was dead and then . . . I just didn't know. . . ."

"They must have known you were going to make it when they left this morning."

"Well. They were right." Francis took a deep breath. "If I've been in this bed two weeks they must have taken my clothes." He raised the thin blanket that covered him and looked under it. "What have they got on me?"

"Well . . ." Lottie blushed.

"What is this? Some kind of wool diaper?"

"Like I said, we've been feeding you broth and meat for two weeks and you couldn't get up. So we had to—"

"Like a *baby*?"

"Well, yes. I guess you could say—"

"Where are my buckskins?"

"Francis, you shouldn't be jumping up—"

"Right *now*!"

Lottie shrugged and went to the corner where the gold pack lay. She brought him his clothing.

"They cleaned them and smoked them so they smell like new-cut pine."

"Turn around. Face the door." Francis sat up—the effort almost made him pass out—and after much struggle and with many pauses to rest, he took the diaper off and got his clothes on. "There. Now, hand me my rifle, would you, please?"

Lottie brought him the rifle. "The gold is safe here too. Anything else?"

"No. Not now. I have to rest again, just for a while. I'll just close my eyes for a few minutes. Just for a very few minutes." He laid the rifle next to him and closed his eyes, opened them and closed them again. Lottie smiled and tiptoed to the door.

"Lottie?"

She stopped and turned. "Yes?"

"I thought I was dead and all I could think of was you and Billy."

She waited.

"I guess we're a kind of family."

She smiled.

"Thank you . . . ," he said.

"It was nothing."

"Yes. It was. And I'll never forget it but now I have to rest, just a little."

"You go ahead. I'll be right out here by the door on my cot."

"Just for a while . . ."

"Just for a while."

And Francis was asleep.

Chapter Eleven

More than once Francis thought that if he hadn't been so set on getting back to his folks he would have stayed in the village.

It was, first, one of the most beautiful places he had ever seen—and he had ridden through the foothills of the Rockies—with a beauty that changed constantly. The butte was perhaps a thousand feet high, jutting up above the prairie with sheer walls, and even close it still reminded him of engravings of European castles he'd seen in books.

Up the north side there was an angled road—really a wide trail. It was too narrow for a wagon but two horses side by side could traverse it easily, although that didn't matter because the people in the village neither used nor kept horses. Except for this trail it was virtually impossible to reach the top of the butte.

And on the top the village had been built all around the edge to match the butte so that the outside walls of the houses went straight to the edge of the butte and there were no windows or doors on the outside. Anybody who tried to climb the butte to attack would simply run into the walls and not be able to go farther up.

And the houses lent themselves to the beauty. They were made of adobe bricks covered with reddish mud, and their walls were gently curved so that even when they went two and three stories high they seemed to grow directly out of the ground—almost as if they had been not built so much as planted and grown.

In the center of the buildings was a clearing about a hundred yards across and toward the center of this area were three underground houses with curved roofs that rose slightly above the ground. These were the only houses Francis and the children were not allowed to enter.

"Billy says they're called kivas," Lottie told him the first morning he could walk around and see the town. "It's where they have their church and outsiders are not to go there."

It was not a hard rule to obey, considering it was the only rule. Francis had never seen people so happy or so lacking in anger or frustration. Everywhere he turned he met a smile or a nod or a hand holding out a piece of meat or a thin piece of corn bread or a gourd with soup or water in it.

These Pueblo Indians talked a great deal among themselves but were so courteous that as soon as they saw that Francis and Lottie couldn't understand their spoken language they talked mostly in sign language.

Francis knew some of their symbols, because Plains Indians also spoke a great deal with their hands, and many of the symbols were the same. Soon Francis was able to understand and explain the village to Lottie. Billy could have done it too, since he spoke at about a five-year-old's level, but he was never around. Indeed when Francis first saw him Billy seemed to have become Indian. He was naked except for a clout around his waist and he had a quiver of arrows over one shoulder and a bow in his hand, with the sword carried by a thong over the other shoulder.

Billy had changed. When he saw that Francis was recovering he stood on one leg and nodded and said, "I thought you were going to the spirit world. It is good you are not."

The people in the village lived primarily by farming. There were fields at the base of the butte, irrigated by a ditch system. It had been designed with a system of ingenious gates that brought water to all the fields.

They farmed corn, beans and squash. They ate the squash as it came ready and they dried the corn and beans to eat through the winter and while none of the people were fat, none were starving either. Francis had never seen healthier people.

It was true they didn't have horses, but they didn't seem limited by that. They did hunt in the scrub forest north of the butte—mesquite and pine and cedar—and here they found many deer and turkeys and uncountable rabbits. They hunted with short, strong bows that were so powerful they sometimes drove an arrow completely through a deer and out the other side.

Whenever there was a job to do—as when they got the fields ready to plant or replastered the walls of a house with mud—everybody chipped in. As he grew stronger on the diet of turkey and rabbit and corn and cooked beans, Francis worked with them, and so did Lottie and Billy.

It was nearly spring and there was much work to do. The fields had to be prepared for planting, which involved using wooden hoes to break the soil and make soft mounds for the seeds. The irrigation ditches had to be cleaned and repaired.

In the beginning the work seemed like drudgery to Francis, but after a short time he found himself liking the strain on his muscles. It was nearly two weeks since he'd regained consciousness and his shoulder was completely healed except for a small lump where they had cut across the fang marks so the poultice would draw. Now and then he felt a small ache, but it was nothing, and he became strong again working in the fields and on the ditches. He had also made a corral for the six horses—he was afraid to let them graze freely or on a hobble because he didn't want to lose them—and at least twice a day he went down to the corral and fed and rode them and led them to water.

He found himself staying with the horses more and more, and finally he realized that the north was calling him. It was time to get moving if they wanted to get north and cut into the Oregon Trail. Still, he had found a new kind of peace here and loved life in the village. Lottie and Billy seemed happy too, so he kept quiet about moving until he was alone one day with a man who had become his particular friend.

His name was Kashi and he was about thirty-five years old—considered an elder in the village—and sometimes at night they would sit by the fire and hand-talk. Francis had tried to tell Kashi about the Plains tribes, how they lived and hunted, and about getting away from the Comancheros. Kashi had told him of the history of the village, how the butte had kept them isolated from the Spanish so they still lived the old way.

But this day they were by the ditch and Francis stopped raking and studied some clouds to the north. Kashi came up to his side and made a sign of birds flying north and pointed at Francis.

Francis nodded and mimicked the sign.

One more sun, Kashi signed, then you go? To-morrow?

And Francis knew it was the truth. He nodded. Tomorrow. The horses were so fat on spring grass they looked greasy; the days and nights were warm; Lottie had made good new moccasins for them, and two new buckskin shifts for herself and a buckskin shirt for Billy, though he rarely wore it.

Tonight, then, Kashi signed, you must all come to my house and we'll feast on rabbit and deer and bread.

Francis nodded and smiled and rubbed his stomach and made signs that he would tell Lottie and Billy. But his mind was already on the horses, what had to be done, the gear to be made ready, food and gold and silver to be packed . . .

He was still in the pueblo but his thoughts were gone, heading north.

Chapter Twelve

It was evening. Francis pulled the pinto up on the edge of a small rise and looked back on his little caravan and smiled. They were close to thirty miles from the butte and it was well out of sight. They had come into the juniper and rolling hills—a whole new country.

But there had been a few moments when Francis thought he would never get away from the village.

The feast had been wonderful. Kashi's wife,

named something that sounded like Annas, had baked corn bread in the large earthen ovens outside the houses that resembled beehives and they had venison and rabbit stew and hot bread to dip in the gravy and talked, with Billy translating, until after midnight.

That was when Billy had found out they were leaving the next day.

"I'm not going," he had said as they left Kashi's house and moved back to their own room to sleep.

"Of course you are." Lottie shrugged. "You go where we go, that's how it works. And we're leaving in the morning to find Francis's folks."

"Two Toes said if I stay I can hunt deer with them in the fall and if I get a deer I'll become a man, sort of . . ."

"You're *seven* years old."

"They don't go by years. They go by if you can kill a deer with a bow and arrow."

"No." Francis had shaken his head. "They go by many things. Hunting deer is just one of them. You wouldn't truly be a man for at least five years yet, no matter what Two Toes told you. There are many tests to pass."

"Still, this is a good place to live—"

"You're seven!" Lottie had cut in. "You don't leave your family when you're only seven years old."

"I don't care. I'm staying."

Lottie spluttered, "Billy—how can you *think* of leaving me and Francis? Your own sister! Your own . . ." She looked at Francis. "Francis! You tell him!"

Francis had remembered the stubborn little boy who had sat backward on the mule and hadn't talked for so long Francis thought he *couldn't* talk. I could just tie him up and bring him, he thought, if only he didn't have that sword.

But Lottie solved it. "If you stay here there won't be anything to spend the gold on—there isn't a store for a thousand miles and nothing even *like* rock candy."

"Oh," Billy had said. "Well, then, I'll come with you."

And they had gone at dawn the next morning. They took only four horses, leaving the extra two for the village as a token of gratitude for all the help the people had given. The horses could be ridden, but better yet the horses could pack corn and deer meat up the grade to the village. Until now Francis and the children had been carrying by hand.

The weather had been grand all day, and with all the new clothing and gear and a decent buckskin packsaddle they made good time. Francis let Lottie lead the packhorse with the gold and other equipment and sent Billy off to the sides to hunt with his bow. Billy came back about noon with a huge tom turkey in front of him on the pony, and Francis decided to make camp a bit early so they could clean the turkey and cook it.

He saw a bend in an arroyo ahead, down and to the left, with some large cottonwoods that meant water. There had been rain a few days earlier and it made for good grass for the ponies along the bottom of the arroyo. Francis set up a camp beneath the cottonwood. Billy cleaned the turkey and Francis cut it in strips to cook over sticks above the fire Lottie had started and while the meat was cooking he picketed the horses and then took his rifle and headed out to the west to take a look.

Francis smiled when he saw Billy pick up his bow and sword and head off to the east. Billy was still a boy but in many respects he had grown so fast his actual age almost didn't matter. To take a large tom turkey with a bow was a feat. Turkeys were smart and hard to hunt even with a gun . . . his short time with Two Toes had completely changed Billy.

Francis climbed a ridge on foot and looked back on the camp. He was a half mile away and a quarter mile higher and he moved still higher until he could see for miles to the north and east and west. At first he could see nothing unusual but something caught his eye to the east, a strange line in the scrub forest, and he realized after a moment that it was some kind of road or heavy trail. It came straight from the east but before it came to their campsite it curved away to the north and disappeared in the trees about two miles from the camp.

A trail meant people, and judging by how wide and well traveled this one looked, a goodly amount of people, although he could see no dust.

It was getting close to dark and he moved back toward camp warily. Tempers were still flaring over the war with Mexico, and the Comancheros were somewhere to the south. People moving on the trail might not be friendly. He had just decided that it would be prudent to keep clear of the trail as they made their way north when he heard a twig snap behind him and turned in time for somebody or something to hit him so hard on the side of the head that it seemed his brain was torn loose, and he was completely unconscious before he hit the ground.

"**AHHH, MY DEAR BOY,** we meet again. I must say, though, I didn't think we would again see each other. I had my hopes, not to say dreams. . . ."

Francis swam up slowly from some deep place in his mind.

"You left us in a very sad state, if you'll remember."

He knew the voice but at first couldn't quite place it in his memory. The pain in his head didn't help.

"Imagine our surprise. We were making our way toward that fine trail to see if we couldn't come upon a traveler who would, let us say, help us in our need, when we saw the light from the fire this girl started, and while coming toward the light we found you."

Courtweiler.

And Dubs.

They had come upon him once, before he found Lottie and Billy, and had taken everything he had. He had tracked them and run them down and caught them sleeping and taken it all back, plus their half-dead mule.

"I should have shot you," Francis said. He opened his eyes and tried to sit up but they had him tied wrist to ankle. He stared up at Courtweiler. The little man, in a ragged black suit and top hat, stroked his beard and smiled.

"Yes, my boy, you should have. I won't make the same mistake. What I don't understand is how you seem to come onto such good fortune. This charming girl to cook for you and a veritable fortune in gold and silver. As I think I may have said to you once before, our good luck is your very bad circumstance."

Francis's mind was clearing. The hulking Dubs must have carried him back to the camp—or from the feel of it, dragged him. Lottie was sitting across the fire. There was a welt on her cheek that would soon be a bruise.

Billy. Courtweiler hadn't mentioned Billy. Just

Lottie. Francis craned around and could not see the boy.

"I told them we were on our way back to our family and that they'd come looking for us if we weren't back soon—"

"Hush, child. Or Dubs will strike you again."

Lottie grew quiet.

"Fine. Now, my boy, was there any more gold where you found this?"

Francis didn't answer. Where was Billy? Francis had cast out to the west. The two men had come on him from the west, or maybe the northwest, so they probably hadn't seen Billy. The boy was still out there and might come walking in on them at any moment.

He had to get loose. The two men had turned away to look at the gold and Francis tried his bonds. They were so tight that his hands had gone to sleep, tied with a piece of line from the horse pack, but there was a strand he could feel loosening and he worked at it. He shook his head at Lottie, meaning not to mention Billy, and she nodded, but he wasn't sure if she understood.

"How fortune does change." Courtweiler

turned from the pack. "We were down to eating our shoes again, and on foot, and now we're rich, have a girl we can sell to . . . well, whomever . . . and have horses into the bargain. Honestly, my boy, it's almost worth letting you loose just to catch you again and see what else you can get—"

A whirring went past Francis's face and a stick seemed to pop out of Courtweiler's right shoulder. An arrow! Buried to the bone.

"Arrrrrnnngh!" Courtweiler grabbed at the arrow but before he could pull it out there were more fluttering sounds and three more arrows zipped past Francis.

One hit Dubs in the neck as he was straightening from the pack, the next took him full in the chest and the last one struck him in the stomach.

Dubs reached up and slowly pulled the arrow out of his neck, then actually took three steps toward Francis before he stopped, settled back until he sat, and then slowly went over on his side and lay dead, his eyes never closing.

It wasn't over yet. Francis had been working at getting his hands free the whole time, and he pulled them loose just as Courtweiler jerked the arrow out of his shoulder and started for him, fumbling at his belt for a revolver.

"Francis! Here!" Lottie was up and running. She grabbed Francis's rifle from beside the pack and threw it. Francis caught it, turned and fired without thinking, without aiming, and saw the dust puff out from Courtweiler's coat as the bullet hit his chest and drove him back to fall near Dubs.

Francis pulled the ropes from his legs and felt for his knife at his belt. Gone!

But Courtweiler lay still. It was over. Francis stood there panting and turned and saw Billy beside Lottie.

"Francis!" Billy said. "I saw them, and saw you tied up, and started shooting. I only had four arrows with me. I didn't think, there wasn't time, and then the big one pulled that arrow out of his neck and I thought you were dead for sure! Oh Lord, did I kill him? Just a minute, I'm going to be sick."

Lottie held his head while he threw up and then led him away and held him while he took deep breaths that sounded like crying.

In silence Francis took the sword from Billy's shoulder and started digging two graves back by the cottonwoods, chopping at the sod until he was down to the loose sand beneath and scooping it out until he was far enough down to cover the two men. Then he dragged them over and dropped them into place—after taking the revolver from Courtweiler's belt and a flint and striker from his pocket for starting fires. He folded their arms over their chests and covered them with earth and then with rocks to keep the coyotes out. He didn't feel sorry for them—they would have killed him, after all. But he felt sorry for Billy.

When he was finished he stood over the graves and looked north. He could not see far. It was dark and even the glow from the fire only penetrated a few yards. But he looked north just the same, and thought, Somewhere up there and west a little are my parents.

They would start in the morning when the light was good and Billy was all right. They would start then. It was still a long way and they had seen so many buried from wounds and accidents and cholera and just living, so many, and he hoped there would not be any more graves.

They would start in the morning.

DON'T MISS ANY OF THE BOOKS IN
THE TUCKET ADVENTURES!

THE ADVENTURES BEGIN . . .

Fourteen-year-old Francis Tucket is heading west on the Oregon Trail with his family by wagon train. When he receives a rifle for his birthday, he is thrilled that he is being treated like an adult. But Francis lags behind to practice shooting and is captured by Pawnees. It will take wild horses, hostile tribes, and a mysterious one-armed mountain man named Mr. Grimes to help Francis become the man who will be called Mr. Tucket.

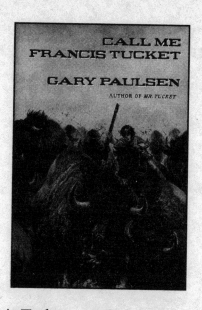

Alone. Francis Tucket now feels more confident that he can handle almost anything. A year ago, on the wagon train, he was kidnapped from his family by a Pawnee hunting party. Then he escaped with the help of the mountain man Mr. Grimes. Now that he and Mr. Grimes have parted ways, Francis is heading west on his Indian pony, crossing the endless prairie, trying to find his family. After a year with Mr. Grimes, Francis has learned to live by the harsh code of the wilderness. He can cause a stampede, survive his own mistakes, and face up to desperadoes. But when he rescues a little girl and her younger brother, Francis takes on more than he bargained for.

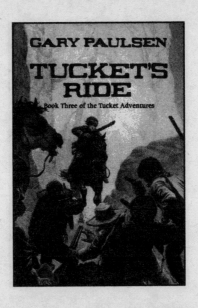

Francis Tucket and his adopted family, Lottie and
Billy, are heading west in search of Francis's parents on
the Oregon Trail. But when winter comes early,
Francis turns south to avoid the cold and leads them
right into enemy territory. The United States and
Mexico are at war, and Francis, Lottie, and Billy are
captured by the most ruthless band of outlaws Francis
has ever seen. The outlaws are taking them away—
away from the trail west, away from civilization, and
away from any chance of rescue.

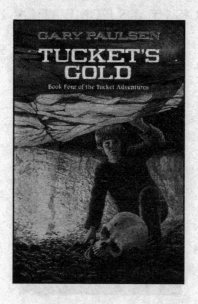

Things look grim for fifteen-year-old Francis Tucket and his adopted family, young Lottie and Billy. Without horses, water, or food, they're alone in a prairie wasteland, with the dreaded Comanchero outlaws in pursuit. Enemies old and new wait at every turn, and death might strike at any moment. But so might good fortune. The three stumble upon an ancient treasure and use teamwork, courage, and fast thinking to hold on to it. When they discover a hidden village, the West doesn't seem so wild after all.

FRANCIS HEADS HOME AT LAST. . . .

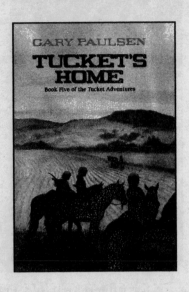

Francis Tucket and his adopted family, Billy and
Lottie, have survived hair-raising and rip-roaring
adventures as they have struggled west, held together
by their goal to find Francis's family on the Oregon
Trail. They also share a secret: the treasure hidden in
their saddlebags. Now the three meet up with a
British adventurer, with men of faith and hope, and
with bloodthirsty ex-soldiers. Even here, at the end of
the trail, surprises and tragic turns await them.

F. M. BLACK MIDDLE SCHOOL
1575 Chantilly
Houston, TX 77018